Jessica

Jessica

초판 1쇄 발행일 2018년 4월 2일

지은이_ 김학진
펴낸이_ 김동명
펴낸곳_ 도서출판 창조와 지식
디자인_ 주식회사 북모아
인쇄처_ 주식회사 북모아

출판등록번호_ 제2015-000037호
주소_ 서울시 성수동 성수이로18길 31, 103호(성수동2가, 풍림테크원)
전화_ 1644-1814
팩스_ 02-2275-8577

ISBN 979-11-6003-079-2 03810

지식의 가치를 창조하는 도서출판 **창조와 지식**
www.mybookmake.com

Jessica

HakJin Kim

What motivated me in writing this short story is the eyes of the brown poodle that left an impression on me. The poodle, one of my friend's, seemed to seduce me to do something for it when my friend showed me its picture last spring. I was asked about the naming of the dog; I chose 'Jessica.' Since then it had haunted me, and I began to make an outline of this story related with Jessica in which I imagined some humanlike creature.

One

In the backseat of Ellen's car, Jessica stares at a woman through the window. She is waving hands to Jessica for farewell with tears in her eyes. That makes Jessica feel sad and nervous because she won't be able to live with that woman any longer. At the same time Jessica wonders if she can live well with a new master, Ellen, and her family. She tries to feel easy about her new home with positive thinking. Soon, a train of thoughts in the past few years continues in her mind and all her thoughts flash back to the days when she came up with the memory of a man one day after she had been weaned.

Jessica isn't just a dog like other puppies. A man,

who died two decades ago, was reincarnated into a dog; that's Jessica. The first day when Jessica sensed that she wasn't just a simple dog, she just passed the odd reality. However, day by day she could feel this bizarre situation and became irritated from the memory of a man. As days went by, at some point she became used to live with those bygone days and even began to try to resume the memory of that man which had been her past life one by one. As she turned two years old, she almost found out all about her previous self, the man, Andy Graham.

Andy Graham was a tall man with blond hair and blue eyes. He had worked as a junior high school teacher while living with his only daughter, Sue, whom he got from his early marriage that ended in divorce. As a single parent he had never been bothered with his daughter who even went to college where she could commute from home. He loved his daughter, Sue, so much, and never had any relationship with other women. He had been busy by doing activities after work to keep him from being lonely. He often went rock climbing and liked playing tennis and skiing, and his swimming was first-rate. When he died of terminal cancer, he was in his early fifties.

Two decades later he opened his eyes in a basket with other puppies and was named Jessica. Soon Jessica, the man reincarnated, was adopted into a woman. To be a dog was a real shock since she became aware of her past life, but she had no idea what to do with it. She had been dumbfounded at her figure, but had to endure it. While she was exploring the memory of her past, she was desperate for a need to prove herself, but all she could hear was just the dog's reverberant bark. As this chaotic time passed, she gave up hope. Instead, she decided to behave herself as it stood, a female dog, Jessica.

 **Two**

When she comes back down to earth, her wailing former master is lost in sight. Jessica thinks that she won't forget her former master who had taken care of Jessica with all her heart and had to work as a Peace Corps volunteer in a foreign country. After two-hour ride with Ellen who becomes her new master, Jessica arrives at a house where a family of four is living. Ellen, a high school junior, gets off her car and takes Jessica out of the backseat. In the distance, Tom Hansen, Ellen's father, who has played basketball alone sees Ellen's car pull into the driveway and come toward him. He runs to Ellen with excitement.

Ellen exclaims, "Dad! Jessica's here. Look at her."

In Ellen's arms Jessica's looking around her new home and finds her so-called daddy. He seems so pleased to see Jessica, and caresses her head gently.

"Hey. Here you are. I'm your daddy now. We are going to be good friends."

And they all go together through the front door. Soon a middle aged woman, Ellen's mother, comes from the kitchen to greet Jessica. For a flash Jessica recognizes who she is. She is familiar to Jessica at first glance.

Jessica feels dizzy and mumbles, "Gosh, what a surprise! I see my loving daughter, Sue Graham, before me."

Jessica is so overwhelmed by Sue's appearance that she can barely contain her breath. She feels enormous gratitude for a reunion with Sue. As the excitement subsides a little, she feels a bit sorry about her situation when she realizes that Sue becomes her human mom whom she is able to get along with for the rest of her life. But she holds a wish that she will let Sue know the truth and recognize her late father, Andy Graham, some day.

Sue seems excited by Jessica as much as Tom, but she has no time for Jessica because she busies herself fixing lunch for her family and a guest, Ellen's close friend, John. Sue still looks energetic like she used to. While Jessica is looking at Tom and Sue, she feels easy and happy. Looking back upon her past life as a man, Andy, especially when he was about to die, he couldn't close his eyes leaving his good girl who was devastated by her father's last moment. About two decades from then Jessica can be relieved by facing that Sue has made her own loving family, and will take care of her, Jessica, the man reincarnated. Tom, Sue's husband, a tall and healthy middle aged man, who teaches high school literature, has been known as a supportive man in his workplace and his neighborhood. He is always ready to help people anytime and everywhere. So he's welcomed wherever he goes. Brian, Ellen's fraternal twin brother, is on his way home from camping to have lunch with John and his family. Both Ellen and Brian are very optimistic all the time by nature and adventurous so that they never rest at home idling. Everyone in the house looks perfect for Jessica, and this family seems to be the best guardian Jessica can aspire to. All she has to do is to accept this reality happily as a speechless female dog even if she still can't understand why this happens to her.

Jessica sighs, but soon becomes curious about the house how Sue and her family have managed. Jessica runs up the stairs heading toward Sue's master bedroom. She sees the clean room where everything is tidy, and feels warm with the sunlight beam. As she looks around the room, she finds a painting which seems to be done by Sue who teaches middle school art. Beside it, a picture is hanging on the wall. In the picture Jessica can see Andy, a tall blond man who stands next to Sue. They look so happy that Jessica gradually becomes sentimentalized over the memory of Andy and his daughter, Sue. Sue was such a nice girl that she never let Andy down. She never mentioned about why she had her father only because she couldn't remember her mother's existence. Jessica recalls how Andy's ex-wife, Jenny Bacon, left him and Sue. Jenny was an ambitious woman who couldn't let herself live as a teacher's wife raising their daughter. Jenny moved to the big city to have a successful career. It was heartbroken when Andy had no choice but to let her go because he didn't want to be an incompetent man in a big city. While Jessica has been lost in memory for a moment, she hears Ellen call out from the dining room.

"I'll come downstairs, Ellen, bow-wow," Jessica barks.

"Hey, are you done with the house. How does that look to you, Jessica? You have dad, mom, Brian and me."

"Come on. Let's go out in the backyard. I have a ball to play with you."
Ellen leads Jessica to the backyard. Jessica hears birds singing in the cloudless blue sky.

"Catch it!" Ellen throws a soft plastic ball. Jessica is

excited feeling happy with a nice family, especially with Sue. While playing, Ellen seems to check messages every minute and then walks to the driveway to get some reference books from Lisa who comes by. At that point Ellen finds a young man getting off his car parked on the street in front of the house. Ellen waves to him with a big smile. Lisa turns her head to check who's in the back and finds her classmate, John.

"Oh, John's here," Lisa says.

Ellen says, "Yes. We'll have lunch together."

Lisa goes back to her car waving fingers to John. Since Ellen and John become friends, it's the first time ever for Ellen to invite him to have meal together with her family. Either one of them has never asked about family matters. They just share things like hobbies and assignments. The only thing Ellen knows about him is that he stays with his mother and his maternal grandmother. She has been fine with him talking and having fun. And then she invites him for lunch to introduce him as a friend to her family. Her parents have trusted Ellen whatever she does because she never made trouble. In a second John comes to Ellen and seems to be surprised a little.

"What a surprise you have a pretty puppy," John says.

"It happens, huh. I've never expected I can adopt a dog because I couldn't stand being with it for a second," Ellen responds with smile on her face.

"Things change anyway."

Saturday lunch is almost ready to be served for five of them. On the table of the dining room a bunch of flowers taken from their garden gives off scent heightening the smell of the food. Jessica goes near the kitchen sniffing because the smell is so familiar that she can't resist the temptation of talking to Sue, a daughter in her previous life. Sue is decorating the cake with frosted cream and says,

"Jessica, a cute girl. Are you hungry? Let me give you a cookie."

Jessica looks up at her with eyes full of love and then she feels watery eyes. But Sue misses it since she concentrates on making food to please her family and a guest. Being a bit awkward, she turns to the living room where Ellen is with John and her dad.

"Lunch's ready. Come on to the dining room," Sue calls them.

As they sit at the table, Brian arrives home and joins them, and soon introduces himself to John. Sue passes a big dish of T-bone steaks around and then a bowl of seafood tomato spaghetti to share.

"It may sound flattery, but every dish is amazing," John exclaims.

And Jessica has been waiting for a piece of meat in silence.

"Thank you, John. You can come over any time. I don't know what to say, but you look familiar to me. Were you brought up in this neighborhood?" Sue asks.

John responds, "Yes, I was born in this town and grew up here up to now. I live with my mom and her mother, my grandmother."

"My mother works for a law firm as an attorney. My grandmother was a lawyer, too. But I think I'm gonna be a painter."

Tom says, "To me, you look like a poet. But, don't take it seriously."

"As a literature teacher I'm saying like that. I remember you got an 'A' in my class, right?"

John says, "Yes. Mr. Hansen."

"Brian. I remember you because I bumped into you several times."

Brian says reluctantly, "Yeah. I guess so. I used to be hurry for the class. So I don't see anyone before me."

"Do you have any writer to talk about?" Tom asks.

"I was impressed with your writing for the school paper."

"Oh Dad, please don't talk about that. Brian. How was your camping? Don't say that I ruined it. You must have left your friends behind to have lunch with John,"

Ellen says.

"Tell me about it. But it's not that bad to be with John. John! Don't be sorry," Brian says.

"Yep, I appreciate your saying so," John says.

"At night in the woods I was afraid that a grizzly bear would appear and attack us," Brian says.

"Because I heard there had been a serious attack so that a man died. Surprisingly, he didn't have any protection tool like pepper spray."

"What a horrible accident it was. I can't believe it. I thought bears rummaged through the garbage can," Ellen says.

Tom, as a wine lover, seems elated while sipping the wine. He's second to none when it comes to drink. Meanwhile, putting her head down on the floor near Ellen's chair, Jessica is bored listening to people's meaningless conversation. She is only waiting for a piece of meat feeling lonely because no one in the room seems to care about her this time. All of sudden, Jessica smells beef at hand and finds a piece of meat on

John's palm. She licks his palm after eating it. As their conversation lapses after couple of hours, Brian stands up checking messages on his cell phone and Sue begins to clean the table. Tom takes the wine bottle with the glass and sits on the couch to watch a baseball game.

John and Ellen make their way to the backyard after Jessica. Jessica runs ahead feeling relieved. At some point she stops to sniff the grass and rolls onto her back rubbing slowly her head. She says herself, "Hmm, how soft it is. I love this kind of grass. This backyard is cozy. I like that. Anyway everything in this home is perfect for me and Sue, and grandchildren."

Beside Jessica, John bends over a bunch of violet flower and says, "I love to see purple things. How about you?"

"Well, I don't know. Believe or not, those who love dark purple color have cynical character," Ellen says.

"Anyway everybody has different taste in color."

"Are you taking swimming class during the summer break?"

John asks, "Why?"

Ellen says, "I don't think you're good at swimming. I think you'd better improve it so you won't be picked on by Jeff."

"I don't care. Why should I care, huh?" John grumbles.

Ellen gives a shrug of the shoulders. She still has no idea why she should treat John like her younger brother though they are in the same year. She has watched his back since John and Ellen became friends.

"Hey, do you have time for now?" John asks.

"Yeah, why?" Ellen answers.

"I wanna show you where I spent my childhood if you'd like to see," John says.

"I think I'm exposing myself to you," he mumbles.

Ellen and John hop in John's car and Jessica slides across the backseat. Jessica watches her neighborhood pass by the window thinking of her past life. In the state of Georgia where Andy, her previous self, grew up, the weather was not harsh so that tall trees and woods appear in the neighborhood along the winding roads.

He loved to drive along the forest path. In the leafy suburbs, Andy and Jenny Bacon raised their baby, Sue. One year after Andy got a job as a P.E. teacher and Jenny graduated from college, Jenny abandoned her home leaving Andy and Sue, a two year old baby. Jenny went up to the north. From then on, Andy had never seen Jenny.

Three

About twenty minutes later John pulls his car in front of a mansion. Ellen seems to be impressed and says, "Hey, what a surprise. You're living such a big house. Oh. Let me count how many windows I can see."

John says, "Don't be silly, huh. This house is too big for three."

When Jessica starts to run toward the front door as if she deserves to know the house, John stops her and says, "Not that way, Jessica. We'll go round to the back of the house."

There Ellen and Jessica find a fairy-tale tree house.

"John. You amaze me," Ellen says.

John responds, "Really? This is what I wanna show

you. What do you think?"

"Can we go inside?" Ellen asks.

As soon as John nods, Jessica runs up the stairs to reach the door and pushes it. The air that flows through the room deludes Jessica that she breaths in Georgia. Jessica mumbles, "This smell reminds me of a thick forest which is warm and wet."

Ellen exclaims, "Wow. Interior looks even nicer. I can see views of the outside with floor to ceiling windows."

"What's this? Don't tell me you worked on it," Ellen says picking up a knitting bag.

"It's for some wild flowers when I collect them."

Ellen says, "So, this tree house is what you wanna share with me and Jessica. Jessica. Are you looking around to find any goodies?"

Jessica is a bit embarrassed and disappointed because Ellen never seems to try to understand her. To Ellen, Jessica just eats and runs. That makes sense to human being. Jessica doesn't have to take it personally since she's a simple dog.

While Ellen is looking around the room, John walks next to her and says, "You know what? I envied of friends with siblings in my childhood. My mom and granny were very busy at work. I had been always home alone though they tried to devote to me."

"You have no idea how lonely I was when there was no one at a fuss. The home was like an empty temple."

"As you see, I make things like spaceships using Lego blocks and knit when I stay in this room. You can join me here."

Ellen says with a smile, "I'll pass. I'd rather swim. I love to be involved in physical activity. I think we can enjoy swimming or rock climbing together."

John agrees with Ellen that they can find some activity to spend time together. While they are chatting, Jessica feels drowsy and remembers her past life as Andy. Andy's house was located in the dead end street so that a large garden in back of the house was surrounded by the lush forest. In that garden his daughter, Sue, played the ball games with him and painted the forest.

That night at home, sitting on the sofa next to Ellen Jessica feels frustrated with her fate--a dumb dog--but nothing comes to her mind to challenge the fate. As she thinks of herself over and over, she hears Ellen talking on her cell phone. Strangely enough, Jessica can hear John's voice on the cell phone.

He asks, "Hey, are you free this Saturday?"

"Why?" Ellen asks.

"I want to have dinner with you on my mom's birthday."

"Is your mom okay with me? I've never met her."

"Sure. I already told her about you. She was so delighted, you know."

"She says she's wondering how her son's best friend look."

"Oh, then, yes," Ellen says.

"What do you have in mind for the birthday present?" Ellen asks.

John says, "Well, flower will be fine. Don't bother, please."

"I'll pick you up at 5 o'clock. She booked for four at a fine restaurant."

"Then I think I have to leave Jessica at home," Ellen sighs.

"No no. You can come with her. There's a lounge for puppies," John says.

Ellen says, "That sounds great. Jessica will love it. She likes the pet lounge."

"Before we join the dinner, I need to get permission from my mom."

On Saturday Ellen and Jessica step out onto the small porch and make their way toward John's car. Ellen climbs into the passenger seat holding a floral bouquet and Jessica slides into the backseat, and the car pulls away. They hit the road, and Jessica watches the city pass by the window, which looks like soulless concrete blocks. They cross the city and go past the recognizable modern building. And then they arrive on time at the restaurant which is located inside the country club in the suburbs. John and Ellen approach the club house to ask about the dog's lounge.

"Oh no! This is not what I expected. I thought I could see John's family. What the hack! I have to stay with other dogs. Huh!" Jessica growls.

But they don't sense what Jessica thinks, and put her in the lounge. Jessica can't help getting interested in the new place, and joins other dogs in the lounge.

As John and Ellen get in through the revolving door, they are guided to the table by the window. They cross the floor which is placed for dance in case of the band's playing the music. John smiles at his mother and his grandmother and introduces them to Ellen.

John says, "Ellen, this is my mom."

"Nice to meet you, Mrs. Greiner. Thank you for inviting me to your birthday dinner," Ellen says.

"Call me Kate. I'm very happy to have you here, Ellen. I've heard of you a lot," John's mother says.

When Ellen turns her eyes to John, she notices John blushes a little bit.

"And this is Jenny Bacon, my mother," Kate says.

"Hello. Nice to meet you, Ms. Bacon," Ellen says.

"Call me Jenny. Nice to meet you, too."

"You look gorgeous. I mean it," Ellen says.

"Thanks. I'll take your compliment," Jenny says with a smile.

Kate laughs and says, "Ellen, today is my birthday."

Ellen is abashed at that moment, but quickly says, "Oh. You're pretty, Kate. You look like in your thirties."

John giggles when he hears women's talks at the scene of their first meeting. As they talk about what has been going on around them so far without any defenses, the birthday dinner seems to be like a family gathering. Jenny and Kate are wondering if John will move to another city which Ellen may live in to attend a college because they seem to stick together all the time.

John says with a wide smile, "Oh, mom, there's still more than a year to go."

After they finish a big dinner, they all go to the lounge to pick up Jessica. When Jessica is called by Ellen, she happens to see Jenny.

"Oh my God! Who is that woman? Is she Jenny? She is an old woman with grey hair, now. But she's still beautiful," Jessica sighs.

"Hey, Jessica, Here I am. Were you okay? Did you have friends here? Now it's time to go home," Ellen says.

And then Ellen says again raising Jessica's forefeet, "Jessica! Say 'hi.' This is Kate, John's mother and this is Jenny, his granny."

Jessica stares at Jenny's face without glancing at Kate and tries to reach Jenny to feel her by making eye contact. She looks at Jenny in the eye with love for a while to show who she was in the past. Being unaware of Jessica's stare, Jenny seems to be interested in Ellen more than a dog.

At last Jenny turns to Jessica and says, "Oh, now I see. This is Jessica. She looks like saying something.

What is it? Honey."

"It's me. I'm Andy. Can you believe this?" Jessica says over and over in her head.

Ellen observes her and says, "Hey, Jessica, you like Jenny, huh. But it's time to let her go. We can see her around soon."

On the way home Ellen becomes curious about Jessica's behavior because she fixed her eyes keenly upon Jenny and looked very serious. She hasn't behaved like that as far as Ellen knows.

"What is it? What makes Jessica stare like that?" Ellen says to herself.

Although she is just a dog, Ellen couldn't stop thinking of Jessica doubting there is something in Jessica.

Meanwhile, Jessica still can't believe how this crazy thing happens--reincarnated and encountering Jenny--but no one knows who Jessica was in the past. After Jessica finds that Jenny has lived well with her second daughter, Kate, from her second marriage and seemed forgetting Andy's existence and Sue, her first daughter, Jessica even feels some kind of sadness. She can't sleep that night because this whole situation is too much for her to bear as a dog. At the dawn of the next day, she runs out to the house that John took Ellen and Jessica several days ago. Even if she knows that her rushing into that house is meaningless now, she just wants to smell the air Jenny breaths. Andy hadn't forgotten Jenny, his ex-wife, until he died because she was his lifetime lover. Jessica inhales deeply deluding herself into thinking that young Jenny is coming with a soft smile. For a few minutes Jessica stays still and then runs back home before Ellen gets up for school.

Since then she runs there every night after checking every member of the family falls asleep, only to see Jenny through the bedroom window in the distance. Day by day she loses her appetite and stays in her bed all day doing nothing. She sighs every minute, just drinking water. She becomes depressed more and more thinking that she's a mere speechless dog and her life is worthless. As days have passed, Ellen begins to feel that something goes wrong with Jessica and tries to pay attention to her. But she has been out for most of the day so that she can't find out what makes Jessica look depressed. And still, Jessica sneaks out to watch Jenny every night. One night Jessica doesn't notice John who finds her while he is parking on the street.

John says with surprise, "Oh. Jessica. What are you doing here tonight? How could you reach here? Are you running away from Ellen?"

As soon as John texts to Ellen who's never expecting where Jessica is, he takes Jessica home before too late. Ellen's been waiting for Jessica and takes over her from John. She tickles Jessica giving her favorite goodies instead of scolding.

Ellen says to Jessica glancing at John, "What a surprise. John found you there. I'm curious about what you were thinking."

Jessica keeps her mouth shut without looking at Ellen. Ellen puts down Jessica nice and easy. After John closes the front door, Jessica climbs upstairs to take a rest. At night she wakes up and feels something, and flash of inspiration comes to her mind.

"That's it. I know how to write though I can't speak," Jessica mumbles.

"First, I have to eat for energy. And then practice drawing alphabet with my legs."

"Oh. You nut! How couldn't you think of this? Your body is a dog, but your mind is Andy," Jessica says to herself. "Okay. Let's try."

Jessica lifts her forelegs and drags them to make a vertical line and then horizontal and circle. She practices drawing lines all day when she is home alone. Now the feeling of lethargy is replaced with exhilaration. She makes progress working bit by bit, one step at a time. When she lifts one foreleg to make a letter, it's not that simple as she thinks. So first she stands on her four legs and then make one foreleg push forward with other three legs anchored on the floor. After getting used to drawing lines, she moves on to the next step: writing a word. It was painstaking job because she has to use only her palms. She doesn't care how much hard she has to try. She just works hard to let Sue and Jenny know that their Andy is with them.

Seen from a distance, she looks like dancing, pacing back and forth. One day Ellen gets home early, but Jessica doesn't notice it while doing her job hard as usual. Ellen sees Jessica, thinking that she's spinning round and round. At a close range she finds Jessica's only one foreleg is moving up and down.

"Jessica. Are you dancing with one leg? Where did you learn that step?" Ellen asks.

And she turns on the music to amuse Jessica while heading to the kitchen to get some drink. Jessica follows Ellen to stop her. There Jessica shows that she can draw 'H' by moving her both forelegs tied together. With no visible trace, it looks like a mime, but Ellen doesn't miss what Jessica is doing. She realizes an odd reality that a dog makes a letter by moving her legs.

"Oh. That's amazing. You know the letters like us?"

"Are you genius? Who taught you? How could you know you can make this letter?" Ellen shouts with surprise.

But soon Ellen gives Jessica a suspicious look and asks her to write another one to see if she really can draw a letter. Jessica begins to write capital letter 'A' because she knows it's easier to make a straight line than a curvilinear one. Ellen seems to be shocked by Jessica's exact understanding alphabets. At that point Sue comes back home from her workplace, a junior high school. She looks exhausted but smiles to Jessica and Ellen who has been making a fuss about the puppy.

"What the noise is it?" Sue asks.

"Is there something wrong with Jessica?"

"I guess she knows alphabets," Ellen says.

"It doesn't make sense. She's just dancing with music. Can you go to the market to get some carrots for me? I just remember them now. Thanks!" Sue says.

And then she walks up the stairs to take a rest for

a while. She lies down on the bed in her clothes, eyes wide open thinking about her ideas for the painting which is scheduled to be displayed in the exhibition room of the school where she's been working as an art teacher.

"How about a landscape with rough brush stroke?" "Or an abstract figure painting? No, no. Too boring," Sue mumbles.

All of sudden something flashed in her face. "That's it. The subject is going to be related with Jessica." She comes downstairs and looks for Jessica. And she finds Jessica in the kitchen that is doing things with her legs.

"Jessica. What are you doing? Stop doing that. You look so weary. Have some cookies, honey." Sue holds her up and kisses her on the head. Even if Jessica feels comfortable on her lap, she gets down on the floor to practice writing. And Sue turns to the fridge to prepare supper. Once a while she looks around the kitchen to check what Jessica's doing and sees her move her legs.

"Hey. I'm gonna put a large paper on the floor for you and make shoes to see what you're doing."

"You are gonna be happy with that," Sue says.

The next day Sue buys a large paper and makes a kind of shoes for Jessica. They look like small socks with strings which keep them from coming off. Sue puts socks on Jessica's four feet. Now Jessica can show what she draws on the paper since Sue designs small socks with washable paints on them so that the line can be visible as Jessica's feet move on the paper. That idea seems amazing enough to satisfy Sue's curiosity about Jessica's motion.

Sue smiles at her and goes to her studio next to the kitchen. Jessica follows Sue and sits down on the paper which becomes her playground, barking and swaying her tail. But Jessica sits crouched near Sue and then falls asleep with shoes on. Meanwhile Sue's been thinking about her painting how she can describe

Jessica in her painting. She begins to sketch Jessica's motion and curvilinear lines which she remembers. At that moment the phone rings in the living room. Sue's startled because she's been absorbed in her work. She stands up and goes to the living room in a flash. She picks up the phone with her pounding heart. She hears Tom over the phone. Tom's voice is shaking because he's nervous.

"Sue, I have a car crash. It's not serious, but it takes time to be finished and I need a ride."

"At the traffic light my car was hit from behind by another car," Tom says.

"Oh. I'm sorry to hear that. Are you okay? I'll be on my way," Sue says.

Sue checks Jessica is still sleeping. Then she grabs the key to the car and goes out the back door and gets into her Chevrolet. A while later as Jessica wakes up and can't see anyone at home, she steps on the paper and starts to practice writing letters. She's already wearing socks which will help her leave marks everywhere she steps on. She lifts forelegs to make a letter and presses and drags. But the hind legs with socks make another stain. She's at a loss for a moment and thinks that she'd better wear socks only for forelegs. But it seems to be impossible to take them off by herself because of strings around her ankles. She has no choice but stay put if she doesn't want to stain the floor, let alone the paper. She decides to sit at the corner of the paper to keep the floor clean.

At dusk Tom and Sue come home.

"It's nice to see you guys," Jessica mumbles.

But they don't look okay.

Tom says, "I really don't understand how that car wasn't insured."

"My insurance has to cover the damage. And then my insurance premium will go up," Tom grumbles.

"Honey, don't be mad at him. How about having a pity on him? He couldn't afford insurance." Sue pats Tom on the back.

Jessica feels that Sue still has a warm heart for

people. She thinks Tom is a nice man, and Sue is even nicer.

Soon, "I'm home," Ellen shouts.

At the supper Ellen is busy talking about how her day was in school. And Brian says nothing but listening to her. Tom and Sue also have been quiet without mentioning the crash. Tom seems to be moved by Sue who doesn't care about the accident, but has sympathy for poor people.

Night falls and everybody goes to bed and Jessica, too. Around midnight Ellen gets up and checks her cell phone. Jessica hops on the bed and reads the message together with Ellen, though Jessica can't catch up with every single word.

It is John who texts the bad news to Ellen.

He texts, "Ellen, I don't know what to do. My mom said her mother was diagnosed with stage 4 terminal cancer."

"I can't sleep. I feel so bad now. I've been happy

with my granny. She spared her free time for me when I was a child. She was an outgoing woman. I don't know why this happens to her." Ellen's face becomes screwed up in surprise when she checks the message. Ellen is absent minded for a few minutes and can't come up with any words. She is the only one whom John may express his thoughts to. She thinks that he wants a friend to share the sad news of his grandmother becoming ill.

Ellen texts, "Do you want me to be with you now? I can go to your place with stuff for school."

"No. But I appreciate your saying so," John texts.

"John. I'm so sorry for Jenny. When did she know this?" Ellen texts.

"She visited doctor two weeks ago. She felt something on the back. A kind of pain, but it lasted for a few seconds. Sometimes she felt a hot flare on the back while she was jogging," John continues texting.

"Her doctor suggested her to go to the hospital to examine her body and the result came like that. She was so sad that she hid the diagnosis from her daughter until tonight. My mom was very upset after the bad news and she said to me that there would be no hope to survive cancer."

Ellen's heart is broken while reading the text message.

"Well. I feel better now. I'll try to get some sleep. See you tomorrow. Thanks a lot. Ellen," John finishes texting.

Next morning Ellen leaves home early to school. She worries about John and has no idea how she can make him feel easy to go through it. As Ellen approaches her classroom, Tom runs into her who doesn't notice him since she is in a deep thought. Tom pats her on the shoulder. She is frightened when she confronts her father's face.

"Oh my gosh, I didn't see you. Sorry," Ellen says.

"What's wrong with you? Is there any trouble with you? I called you out loud for seconds but you didn't listen to me. What were you thinking over?" Tom asks.

"John's grandmother got cancer. John is worried

about his grandmother so much," Ellen says and enters the classroom.

As Tom proceeds, he begins to look back the days when he met Sue who had been depressed a lot fearing the loss of her father who was about to die of cancer. He experienced how hard it was to see Sue who had been through the moment for the last farewell. For months she couldn't sleep well after her father's funeral. Sue's suffering may be a different story for John since he has his mother. In the evening Tom tells Sue what he heard at school.

She ponders a second and says, "I'm sorry to hear that. John and his mother are going through the same sadness that I went through."

Jessica hears their conversation thinking what they are talking about. John's grandmother is Jenny, and she might be sick or what? Jessica wants to see Ellen at once to know more about what's exactly happening to Jenny. Since the puppy lounge Jessica has not seen

Jenny at all. Jessica wants to run to Jenny's residence to see her, but she has to be cautious not to seen by John. When Ellen gets home she finds everybody's asleep. So she can't help talking to Jessica who's staying up alone for Ellen. Jessica has been dying to hear from Ellen all day long.

"Jessica. What can I do for poor John?"

"His granny has only a few months to live," Ellen says.

Jessica is stunned momentarily. At last everything is clear. "What? You are kidding me!" Jessica shouts to herself.

Ellen seems to hear her.

"Jessica. Are you crying? You look like wailing over Jenny's destiny," Ellen says.

"I'm saying this because you were so happy when you were in Jenny's arms. I'm so sad, too. I'm so sorry for her and John."

Ellen keeps saying, "Is there any idea for his granny? Jenny seems a successful woman. The mansion and her Porche Carrera and her designer clothes tell that she made a fortune a long time ago. So, she has almost everything. Then what can bring her happiness? Tell me, Jessica. Aha! I have an idea. How about you? You can be a joy to Jenny."

Jessica mumbles, "Thanks, Ellen. That sounds a great idea. I'd love to be with Jenny." Jessica begins to sway her tail vigorously. This time she also makes up her mind that she will practice drawing letters harder than ever.

Next morning everyone is out of home. Jessica sits on her bed laying her head on her forelegs losing interest in drawing letters due to her worrying about Jenny. She loses appetite again and stays on her bed waiting for Ellen. She feels inadequate and useless. Time seems to pass more slowly when Jessica waits for Ellen. In the evening, the family gets together at the table for supper. Jessica comes down to the kitchen and sits beside Ellen to hear about Jenny.

Ellen says, "I heard Jenny decided to get chemo

as her doctor suggested by visiting the hospital once a month. She will try every method she can do along with the treatment."

Tom responds, "That sounds good. She needs to be strong to get well. Who knows? She'll be cured."

Ellen continues to talk, "I think she'll take a yoga class and have a diet for the patient as some survived people from cancer."

"She'll spend her time in the woods nearby, walking around her spacious garden."

"She looked calm without any surprise saying that no one lived forever."

Listening to them, Jessica recalls that Jenny was an audacious woman who never feared from anything so that she could make a fortune as a successful lawyer in the big city, Chicago. When Jenny and Andy met and had a baby, Sue, Jenny was no one to depend on after losing both parents in a severe car crash. Jenny had no choice but to live in a youth facility because she had no relatives who wanted to take her to their home. So she was sent to the facility, and she was smart enough to enter a college and met Andy. If Jenny has any fault in her life to be sorry, it may be the running away from first marriage with Andy. By the time Jessica recalls the past that Jenny filed for divorce from Andy who didn't agree to Jenny's ambition, Jessica stops thinking her past life as Andy. She just needs to concentrate on what she can do for Jenny.

Several days have passed and Jessica hears Ellen's calling.

"Jessica! Let's go to Jenny. Maybe she'll be delightful if you show up."

"You know what? John didn't agree that you would stay with Jenny even for a few minutes because she had an allergy to animal hair. So I persuaded him saying a poodle is okay."

Four

At last they enter Jenny's house. Jenny has a big smile on her face. And she hugs both Ellen and Jessica. She looks okay at first glance though there is a bunch of medicine on the kitchen table.

Jenny says, "I'm so glad to see both of you again. I feel great now. Hello, Jessica, cute girl."

"Here are biscuits, honey."

"Ellen, how thoughtful you are! I love puppies, but my allergy doesn't let me keep dogs in my house."

"But I heard from John Jessica would be different. So, I think Jessica can come over to me as often as she can."

Even if Jenny smiles all the time, Ellen doesn't

feel good while she's looking at Jenny's haggard face. After a little while, she calls Jessica that has loitered in Jenny's master bedroom.

Ellen says, "Jessica, it's time to go home."

"Ms. Bacon, we'd better go home for now. I think you need a rest. I'll bring Jessica whenever I have time after school."

Jenny says, "Yep. I'd better take a nap today. I'm tired a little. We'll see tomorrow."

On the way back home Jessica plans how to get to Jenny during the day since she has visited several times before.

The next day the sun rises and it's time to go to Jenny's house. Perhaps Jenny may wait for Jessica to come to see her. So Jessica is in a hurry to run to her. In the bedroom Jenny alone lies flat on her bed like a dead woman. Jessica's blood runs cold. She crawls up Jenny's bed and smells her licking her hand. An hour after Jessica lies next to her, she opens her eyes.

She says, "Oh, Jessica. You're here again. How can

you come here by yourself? How long have you been with me? I fell asleep because of medicine. You're a sweet girl. You're so caring."

"Now I feel better. Let's go downstairs."

As soon as they get to the kitchen Jenny makes a dish of steak for both. She's seated in the wooden chair and Jessica next to her. It's a fabulous feast to Jessica. All of sudden Jessica feels the past like Andy was having a meal with Jenny.

Checking Jessica's plate, Jenny says, "Jessica, are you done? Let's take a walk!"

Jessica comes back to reality. And she hops down and heads to the door. Jenny and Jessica start to walk side by side to the forest nearby. Since Jenny starts to have cancer treatment, she has reduced her legal burden in her law firm which she established a long time ago.

Since Jessica visits her around 11a.m. every morning, she becomes Jenny's companion sharing many things. As Jenny tells about her life in Chicago, Jessica finds out that Jenny went to law school on a full scholarship and got a job at authoritative law firm. Some years later she established her own firm. She had lived intensely, and yet missed her ex-husband and Sue. But she has never got in touch with Sue. Andy also had never wanted to know about Jenny's life after the divorce since he felt so betrayed by Jenny who focused on pursuing her career in a metropolitan area.

Now as a living creature which happens to get a chance one more time, Jessica becomes aware that it was really stupid for Andy not to follow Jenny. He was too meek to take a risk in his life. It was a wrong choice for both Jenny and Sue.

One morning when Jessica visits Jenny, Jessica draws a letter 'J' in front of Jenny who seems busy making lunch. Jenny doesn't pay attention to Jessica because there is no mark on the floor. While eating Jessica thinks of the socks as a tool to let the letter visible.

After lunch they go out to walk around the big garden in the back of her house.

Jenny says, "This is a lovely garden, isn't it? Jessica.
Since Kevin died of plane crash, I rarely came out from
the house. I was at work or home."

"Kate has always been busy at work like me since

she left her ex-husband who had an affair with his secretary."

"What do you think of me, Jessica? I'm a pathetic and lonely old woman."

"I think I deserve it. Life ends pathetically one way or another. Is that right?"
Jenny's mouth twists into a wry smile. That leaves Jessica heartbroken, but there's nothing she can do for Jenny.

Almost a month has passed since they were together. Oddly enough, Jenny never doubts how Jessica comes to her. She even winks at Jessica for a secret visit when she sees Jessica with Ellen who comes by after school. John and Kate have no idea Jessica stays with Jenny during the day. If they knew it, they would appreciate Jessica's caring for Jenny more than anyone else. Meanwhile Jessica is very careful not to be discovered by Ellen. She is meticulous enough to deceive Ellen, so she always gets home from Jenny's place to say "Hi" to Ellen who is coming from school. It isn't easy for

Jessica to do this visit, but she couldn't let Jenny stay alone feeling lonely.

One day before Jenny is supposed to undergo the third chemotherapy, Jessica thinks she can delay her plan no longer. She has to show what she can do to Jenny. So she takes out her two socks from the cabinet and holds them in her mouth. During the trip to Jenny's house socks are soaked with Jessica's saliva. When she enters Jenny's kitchen through the doggy door, socks are totally yucky. But kind Jenny picks them up to wash in the kitchen sink. Finally Jenny puts washed socks on the floor and says, "Here are things you brought, your socks. Did Ellen make them for you?"

"Oh, you want me to help you put your socks on!"

"Okay, you're done. They're wet. Do they bother you?"

Without any barking Jessica begins to move forelegs to write the word "No." It takes several minutes to finish it because her forefeet don't slip smoothly in wet socks. In spite of Jessica's hard try, Jenny doesn't recognize the word instantly. She just sees a water stain and says, "Oh, you like to play with water. Huh." And then she holds up Jessica to take socks off and let her go out to walk as usual. Reluctantly, Jessica gives up drawing and follows Jenny. This time they walk along the neighborhood and then go into the forest instead of Jenny's garden. Jenny seems to be delightful with quietness in the sizable deep woods.

She says, "This path reminds me of Georgia and my ex-husband, Andy. That's ridiculous!"

And she laughs. After an hour walking they find a white painted bench. Jenny sits down for a little rest since they walk farther than their usual routine. Jenny takes out a bottle of water and pours it in a small bowl for Jessica saying, "Tomorrow is a regular checkup day. You stay your home. I'll be home around 4 o'clock. You can come the day after tomorrow. Okay?"

When Jessica gets home, she checks that no one is home yet. But to her surprise she has been seen on the road by Sue who is on her way back home from school for the day. Sue doubts in her eyes when she sees Jessica walking on the street. As soon as Sue gets inside the house she calls Jessica who is running to her.

"Did you go somewhere? I saw you walking on the street."

Jessica doesn't answer and licks her hands thinking, "I should get home earlier and careful."

The follow morning breaks through the clear sky. Jessica remembers what Jenny said. She'd better stay home since Jenny will go to the hospital to check her condition and to get chemo. She becomes bored, but she has to be patient not to evoke Sue's suspicion over Jessica's action. While wandering the house, Jessica is anxious about Jenny's physical condition.

Jessica mumbles, "To me Jenny seemed to be getting better and better. Anyway it's out of my hand. I just do my best to make her happy."

The night falls and all the family go to bed. Jessica

falls asleep too. In the middle of night Jessica feels something in the room. To her surprise Jenny is coming to her with a happy smile and says, "Andy! Jessica was you. You came back to me. I'm so sorry that I left you and Sue. I should tell you this. I was so selfish, but it was too late to get together. I still love you, Andy. Stay with me forever." Jessica is startled and wakes up. And she remembers that Jenny was dressed in a one-shouldered violet chiffon dress which was a special gift that Andy presented Jenny. Jessica comes to wonder if Jenny still has that dress in her stuff. And all of sudden, Jessica begins to worry about Jenny who might be in trouble. That's why she showed up in Jessica's dream.

At this point Jessica cannot get back to sleep wondering if Jenny is back home or is held in the hospital because the tumor expands into her other organ. If Jenny is held in the hospital, Jessica will spend her time at home. To discover what happens to Jenny it will be easy to check Ellen's cell phone. Jessica reaches her cell and pulls it to fall and presses the message button.

Any dog but Jessica may not do this thing.

She discovers an unread message and opens it. She is almost fainted when she reads it. It reads, "Ellen, bad news again. My grandma fell asleep while she got chemo and then she kept sleeping. The doctor said she might get shocked and was trying to do his best."

Jessica reads more messages that make her heart fall. She sits motionless for a while thinking that Jenny's fate would be in the scale. She can't do anything for her to get well.

She mumbles, "God, I hope Jenny will get well. I'd like her to live longer. And she needs to know how much Andy loved her enough to live without any woman after divorce."

With sadness Jessica stays up all night.

Before Ellen leaves for school, she says to Sue, "Mom, I'll visit Jenny after school to see how she's doing."

"If she's awake and she can be discharged from the hospital, I'm gonna let Jessica stay with her for several days to please her. Is it okay with you?"

Sue answers, "No problem. I'll miss Jessica, though. Oh, don't forget to take her socks. Jessica in socks may amuse Jenny a lot."

In the hospital Jenny has lain in bed with a respiration gadget on her nose. She seems to fight by herself to pull her strength back. She might have been at home to greet Jessica in her dream. When Ellen and Jessica arrive at the entrance of the hospital, they are stopped by a security man because the dog is not allowed to enter the patient's room. So Ellen puts her in the car and goes to Jenny alone. As soon as Ellen sees Jenny lying still without any motion, she comes out from the room and calls John.

She says, "I brought Jessica to show Jenny, but she can't make it right now. And I planned to leave Jessica with Jenny for a while. What do you think of it?"

"That's a great idea," John says over the cell phone.

"The doctor says that she can go home after taking off the respirator because she's not in a coma."

"That's odd, but there's nothing doctors can do for her for now."

Ellen interrupts him and says, "Wait a minute. Isn't that kleine-Levin Syndrome?"

"What is it?" John asks.

"It is known as 'Sleeping Beauty' syndrome. This rare sleeping disorder causes people to sleep more than 20 hours per day," Ellen says.

John asks, "Does it last for the lifetime?"

"I don't know exactly. I heard it lasts from several days to several years," Ellen says.

The next day Jenny's physician releases her after making an appointment for chemo. John sees Ellen and Jessica who have been waiting for him at the door as he approaches the driveway. After Jessica John goes upstairs holding his grandmother in his arms and lays her in her bed. And he calls his mother, Kate.

He says, "Mom. Granny is home now. Jessica will stay with us in our home for a while. Ellen allows Jessica to do that."

Ellen hears Kate's appreciation.

John looks around her room checking everything in order and says, "Jessica. I believe you. You'll take care of my grandma. Thanks."
Ellen says the same words as John.

She adds, "I wanna stay a while, but we have a swimming class today. You can have your meal anytime as much as you want. Bye now, Jessica."

As soon as Jessica sees them step down the stairs, she hops up in Jenny's bed and leans Jenny's arm sniffing her. It is at dusk when Jenny opens her eyes.

Suddenly, Jenny calls, "Andy! Where are you?"
Jessica begins to lick her cheek.

Jenny says, "Hey, it's you, Jessica. I thought you were Andy. I think I'm dreaming."
Jessica stuns for a moment, but wonders if Jenny goes out of her mind.

"Get well! Jenny," Jessica barks.

By the way, Jenny asks, "Can you get me some food, Jessica?"

Jessica is embarrassed a lot to be asked such an errand like that. She doesn't understand how Jenny asks a dog to bring food from the kitchen. But Jessica comes up with an idea. In the kitchen Jessica pulls a chair with full strength to reach the bowl and bites a pear tight and jumps down. As she climbs the stairs, she can feel her mouth watering and drooling on the carpet. At last she drops a pear on Jenny's palm. She babbles with her eyes half closed, "Thanks." And she begins to eat it and then falls asleep again.

For several days Jessica has been with Jenny looking after her. There's not much thing to do for Jenny. Mostly, Jessica practices how to move her forelegs to write alphabets. Watching Jenny who has been sleeping almost 20 hours a day is painstaking for Jessica. But there's nothing Jessica can do to wake her up. While Jessica has watched Jenny from dawn till dusk, she has a chance to look around the house. Everything seems neat and tidy in the big house. After roaming the rooms

Jessica finds out that Jenny still has a violet dress Andy presented. Jessica is so pleased to see that Jenny never forgot Andy. Since then Jessica practices the specific sentence, "I was Andy."

After a month, Jenny opens her eyes wide in the morning and says, "Jessica, I thank you so much for staying with me."

"I think I can hear you what you are saying when you bark. I have no idea how I can understand you when you bark."

It's a real shock to Jessica because Jenny understands her. It means that Jenny must have changed while she has undergone 'Sleeping Beauty' syndrome. Then Jenny gets up vigorously and puts on blue jeans and a white shirt humming.

Turning to Jessica she says, "Jessica, I feel so great. I'm free from cancer."

"I'm not dreaming right now, you know. In my dream you spoke to me as Andy did. How awful it was!"

"Sometimes I felt as if I were floating in the air." Jenny seems so excited with the entire thing that she experienced while sleeping.

She says, "You know the world in my dream was different. People I met there look happy all the time. At some point, you stood before me and said that you were Andy. It sounds ridiculous. Is it true?"

"It's odd, but I think there's another world we can't see with the naked eye."
Jessica barks back, and Jenny looks at Jessica with narrowed eyes.

Jenny asks, "Are you saying you agree with me?"

In that evening, Jenny prepares dinner for Ellen and John and Jessica. At the table they are excited sharing the past days, revealing how much John worried about his grandmother and discovered a new joy after seeing her get well. With excitement Jenny tries to show what happened, and goes on talking how she was doing in her dream believing as if she were a healthy woman. That evening looks like the happiest time in her life.

Everybody in the room wishes that no mishap would befall Jenny ever.

As the night falls, Jenny and Jessica together fall into a deep sleep. The rising sun wakes up Jessica. She checks Jenny first, who still is sleeping safely and soundly. Jessica has waited for Jenny to get up. But Jenny doesn't wake up even in the afternoon.

"There's something wrong with Jenny" Jessica mumbles.

Jessica thinks her sleeping is beyond question. Jenny becomes a Sleeping Beauty again. Jenny has been awake and come around from sleeping just for one day.

That evening Jessica has to be taken to Ellen's home back as Kate installs a surveillance camera. She can't put Jessica in such a desolate house. Almost for a month after leaving Jenny, Jessica has been in hell worrying Jenny so much. All she can do is to practice drawing letters with her forelegs in case Jenny gets her life back on track. Then Jessica will express what's in her mind.

The harder Jessica practices drawing, the more she becomes pessimistic about what's ahead. Whenever she imagines the worst case, she runs to Jenny's house once in a while and watches her bedroom window hoping to see Jenny, but nothing happens, and runs back home.

At last, the day comes when Jenny gets out of Sleeping Beauty syndrome for good. This time things change as Jessica has been afraid of. Jenny doesn't remember that Jessica has been with her for a month. So when Ellen takes Jessica to Jenny, she says, "Hi, cute girl, Jessica. How are you doing?" That is it.

From then on Jenny's normal day begins with her tumor shrunk a lot.

 **Five**

Everything seems excellent for every member of two families. On one Saturday after Jenny has come to herself, Sue and Tom are visited by Kate Greiner.

Kate says, "Hi. I'm Kate. We haven't properly met. I really thank you for your support. My mom gets better and better."

"Here's a token of thanks, a cake and a bottle of wine. Jessica was a good friend for my mom. And Ellen is so nice to John. He really likes to do everything with Ellen. I'm really happy to see John get along with Ellen."

"I'm so grateful to you."

"If you don't mind, I'd like to invite you all to our

house."

Sue answers, "You shouldn't have! But, we'd love to accept your invitation gratefully."

"I heard you're quite busy."

Kate says, "Yes, I'm up to my neck in work and hardly have my time left myself."

"Oh, I should get going now. I'll let John talk with Ellen about the date and time. Thanks a lot. Bye for now."

Then Kate leaves for the office in a hurry.

By the way, Jessica feels abandoned even if she eats a piece of cake which Kate brought for her. She is just a puppy and she can't stand this situation. She weeps whenever she's alone. She has no reason to weep at all if she lives without knowing her previous life as Andy. She wishes that she would forget all the past days. But she has no power to be a normal dog. Jessica is looking back at her which has stayed at Ellen's house for the last five months. Unlike before, she has experienced a lot of things. Consequently, she is under stress of her new life. One day she is sobbing on the floor in agony when Sue comes home early to work on her painting for the exhibition. She sees Jessica lying on the floor.

"Come on, are you okay?"

She pulls her up and takes to her room which has been spared for the art work. She puts down Jessica in the room and spreads a large thick paper on the floor.

She says, "Jessica, this is for you. You can play on the paper. I'll put socks on your feet and then you can draw like before. I'm sure you feel a lot better. Huh?"

Jessica says okay, "Bow-wow, bow-wow."

A little later, both Sue and Jessica seem to concentrate on their works. Sue is working with her apron on and Jessica is wearing socks to draw. While Sue paints an oil painting, Jessica lets her socks soaked in various watercolor pigments to make letters. When they listen to a waltz, Jessica pricks up her ears. It's 'Over the Waves' that Jenny and Andy loved to listen together. Jessica isn't the only one that appreciates it at that moment. Sue also pays attention to that music. Soon Jessica uses her wits to develop her idea to make Sue know who Jessica was. She begins to write a letter 'o' and 'v' and progresses the rest of the word. The word looks like dancing, but it is absolutely a word. Jessica taps Sue to show her letters. Sue turns her face to Jessica and sees some flamboyant drawing. To her surprise, seen from a distance it is a word, 'over the waves.' At first she thinks it is a coincidence, but she realizes that it is a real word. With full of doubtfulness in her eyes, Sue looks back at Jessica thinking how she could know the title of the song. Besides, it was the song that her father, Andy, liked to hear most. More and more Sue becomes suspicious about Jessica. So, she asks Jessica to follow the instruction that she's going to give.

Sue says, "Jessica, one nod means 'no', two nods mean 'yes', Okay?"

Jessica nods twice and Sue jumps at Jessica's responding.

Sue asks, "My dad's name was Andy?"

Jessica nods twice.

Sue says, "Oh my God! Were you my dad?"

Jessica nods twice again.

Sue feels faint and says, "What's happening here?"

"You are a puppy. You were my dad, Andy."

"Does anyone else know this secret?"

About this question, Jessica nods once.

Sue mumbles, "It's unbelievable! Do I have to tell Tom and Ellen this incredible thing?"

At that moment Jessica taps Sue and nods once. And then she shakes her head jumping on the paper making the word 'No.' Soon she draws the words, 'you and me.' All three words are mingled enough not to be readable, but Sue knows what Jessica is going to express. Sue stops doing her painting and sits on the chair with Jessica on her lap. She stares Jessica and realizes that this odd thing is happening before her. Now Sue is with her dad whom she has missed so much since he was gone.

Sue sits still for a while to put herself together, and then says to Jessica.

"Do you know Jenny?"

"When I heard Ellen would like to put you in Jenny's house because you liked to stay with Jenny, I was curious because I thought you just saw Jenny once at the restaurant."

"Okay, let me ask you. Do you know her? If yes, nod twice."

Jessica nods twice.

"Was she your lover when you were Andy?" Sue asks.

Jessica nods once.

"Then who is she?"

Jessica stays still, and quiet. Sue doubts who is Jenny to Jessica.

All of sudden Sue figures out what's happening. Her late father is reincarnated into a dog with all the previous memory. That's why Jessica behaved so oddly since she arrived at her house. She recognized Sue as soon as she saw and licked Sue's hand with emotion.

As Sue finds that Jessica doesn't like to give the truth about Jenny, she stops questioning.

And Sue tells Jessica that she'd better keep painting. Sue looks down the paper on the floor which is filled with various hues of strokes and unreadable letters along with vivid letters. It is a real art piece by the look of it.

Sue says, "You must be proud of you, huh. It looks like an Expressionist painting."

Jessica mumbles, "Thanks" by drawing the letter 'tha'.

After that afternoon Sue sees Jessica as her cute pet as well as her late father Andy.

The day comes when Jessica can see Jenny in her house. Jessica plans to do what has been in her mind. Worryingly, that may be shocking news to Sue and Jenny. On the other hand, Sue also has made up her mind what to do about Jenny and Jessica.

Five of them stand in front of the grand door. Kate and John greet them at the door. Jenny stays in the kitchen with the household servant to check everything in order. Tom's family is guided to the dining room where displays valued pieces of china in a glass-fronted golden cabinet. Jessica is also seated on the chair between Jenny and Ellen.

Jenny as the oldest one speaks first.

"I'm very happy to have all of you here. I wanna thank you, Mr. and Mrs. Hansen for everything. And Ellen did a lot of things for me. I really appreciate it."

"And Jessica! You were the best one for me," Jenny says and pats her smoothly.

Tom says, "We are very happy to see you get well. Ms. Bacon. And I wanna thank you for inviting us here."

"As a wine lover, I appreciate your serving this top-quality wine. What a great taste it is!"

"And you have a beautiful big house," Tom says.

Jenny smiles at Tom and says, "Thank you. You can come over any time from now on to talk about literature."

Tom says, "You heard of me from John. Yes, I'd love to talk about works, especially, about Poe's novels."

"I heard you've worked dealing with legal matter. You sound like you're interested in the literature"

Jenny says, "Yes. I like to read novels."

She is gazing at Sue and then says, "I heard Sue is painting a big piece for the exhibition."

As Jessica hears their conversations, she worries about Sue. Even if Sue is in her mid forties, she will be shocked by encountering her biological mother. She may have never imagined that mother and daughter can hold their first reunion in forty five years. Jessica doesn't feel at ease.

The lunch is almost over. Brian becomes interested in John due to John's belongings like a yacht. Three of them go out for movie and Kate's out too. Tom rises to his feet after getting a message.

Tom says to Sue and Jenny, "Oh. I'm sorry I should go now. One of my neighbors needs to get help."

"Sue, are you gonna stay longer? I'll pick you up in two hours."

Sue says with a smile at Jenny, "Yeah, pick me up

after finishing it."

In the end, there are only Jessica and two women left in the house. They move to the living room to get some more coffee.

Jenny asks to Sue, "How long have you lived in this neighborhood?"

Sue says, "Almost ten years."

"Excuse me. Ms. Bacon." Sue turns to Jessica and says, "Hey, Jessica. I think you have something to show me and Ms. Bacon." Sue winks at her. Then Sue asks Jenny a piece of big paper and put socks on Jessica's forefeet.

Sue says, "Jessica, can you write your name, please?"

Jenny watches them with curiosity. Jessica begins to make letters 'Andy.' Jenny is so startled that she almost flies out of her skin.

She cries out, "Andy? My ex-husband? It's impossible. How does she know his name?"

Sue explains what happened about a week ago and she couldn't believe this situation. But she finds out her dad, Andy, is reincarnated into a dog, Jessica.

"What?" Jenny's eyes popped in surprise.

Sue says, "Jessica expresses herself by writing with her feet. She knows how to write because she remembers everything about the past days when she lived as Andy."

Sue adds: Jessica is quiet when she is questioned about Jenny. She continues to say that she's curious why Jessica doesn't tell her about Jenny though she cares for Jenny a lot. Jenny listens to Sue prudently, and finally begins to gaze at Sue with mixed emotion.

After a few minutes, a flood of tears streams down from Jenny's eyes and says, "Honey. It's you, my little girl, Sue."

"I know I have no right to call you my daughter since I left you and Andy."

"You can't forgive me, can you?"

And then she begins to weep hard.

Sue seems shocked and says, "What? Are you my mom? You're kidding me. Is it true? Jessica?"

Jessica nods twice. Sue is struck dumb.

Sue asks in resentment, "I thought I had no mother while I grew up. Andy never mentioned of my mother. He didn't put any photos of her around me."

"But how couldn't you try to find your own flesh and blood?"

Jenny says, "I'm so sorry. I was out of my mind to make my career. I worked really hard and got a chance to start my own law firm."

"I missed you a lot, but things didn't let me have you."

Jenny looks down at Jessica with eyes full of tears and says, "It was Andy, huh. Jessica was Andy."

She calls Jessica Andy. "Hi. Andy."

Jessica nods once. Sue instantly reacts to Jenny.

"Don't call her Andy. She doesn't want to be called like that. She's Jessica now. She just remembers her past life."

Jenny says, "All right, I've got it. By the way, can you forgive me, Sue? I know it'll take time."

Quiet mood falls for a while and Sue says, "It's the past. It is grateful to have Jessica and have a mother."

Sue is still a warm-hearted woman. Jenny hugs Sue and kisses her on the cheeks.

Jenny says, "You have my eyes like Kate. So when I saw you at the table, I thought ironically you might be my baby, Sue."

"I'm extremely happy. I could see you before I die."

Sue says, "Don't even think about it. We band together at last. I'm so happy, too."

"Jessica! Dad! Thank you. Now I have mom and a half sister."

After listening to their conversation, Jessica begins to draw 'Jenny' and it takes a while to finish it.

Jenny screams, "Oh, Andy, you remember me. How thoughtful you are!"

Jenny looks excited by looking at her name, a water stain on the floor and her daughter, Sue. Now Sue and

Jenny share one secret; Jessica is a dog with Andy's soul. Two women agree to keep their mouths shut for some time.

As the day for the exhibition is coming near, Jessica works day and night to finish the painting which comes from Sue's idea that Jessica's footprints will be a great painting. On the paper Jessica writes letters by drawing and jumping here and there. And then the paper comes out to be a piece of art work solely for Sue, not for herself. On the opening day of exhibition, people are amazed at the Jessica's work.

There are so many words overlapped and juxtaposed. People in the room ask Sue how the dog can make letters. In the end the painting gains a great media attention in the state, so her work airs on the morning news. Since then, Jessica enjoys her fame for a certain period of time by running into some photographers who have been waiting to take pictures of her when she walks out the front door.

Now Jessica feels something like the next chapter of her life.

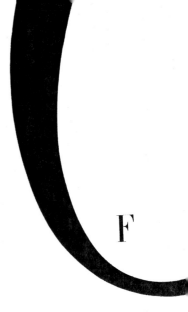